Hodder
Children's
Books

A division of Hodder Headline Limited

WHEELIE GIRL

MIRIAM LATIMER

'I CAN'T DO ANYTHING,'

Molly cried,
as she sat alone in the corner.

'I can't skip,

or swing,

or kick a football,'
said Molly sadly.

'I always
end up in a
muddle.'

Just then, a beautiful butterfly came
and sat on Molly's hand.

'What's the matter with you?'
said the butterfly to Molly.

'I can't do anything properly

because I have wheels for feet,'
said Molly.

'Everyone can do something,'
said the butterfly.
'You just have to find out what it is.'

And she danced off into the breeze.

'Hmmm,' thought Molly.
'I must be good at something.'

And with a spin in her wheels
she went to find out
what it was.

Under a row of very tall trees,
Molly spotted Archie Davis,
swinging from branch
to branch.

'I can climb trees too,'
said Molly.
She scrambled up the trunk,
and fumbled and slipped

through the leaves until,

eventually, she reached

the top

of the tree.

'I'VE DONE IT!'

she shouted.

But
just then
a jackdaw
who loved to collect shiny objects
spotted Molly's
wheels glistening
like jewels in the sun, and he
swooped down to collect his treasure.

He clasped Molly's wheels and
carried her off to his nest.

'No, no, this will not do,' said Molly.

'I can't climb trees with shiny wheels.'

As she passed the harbour,
Molly noticed Matilda

gliding between the boats.
Matilda could swim as skillfully
as a **dolphin**.

'I
can
swim,'

said Molly.

'The butterfly was right.'

And she dived into the water

splashing

and spluttering

around the boats.

But just then
a fisherman
hooked one of
the spokes
of Molly's
wheels.

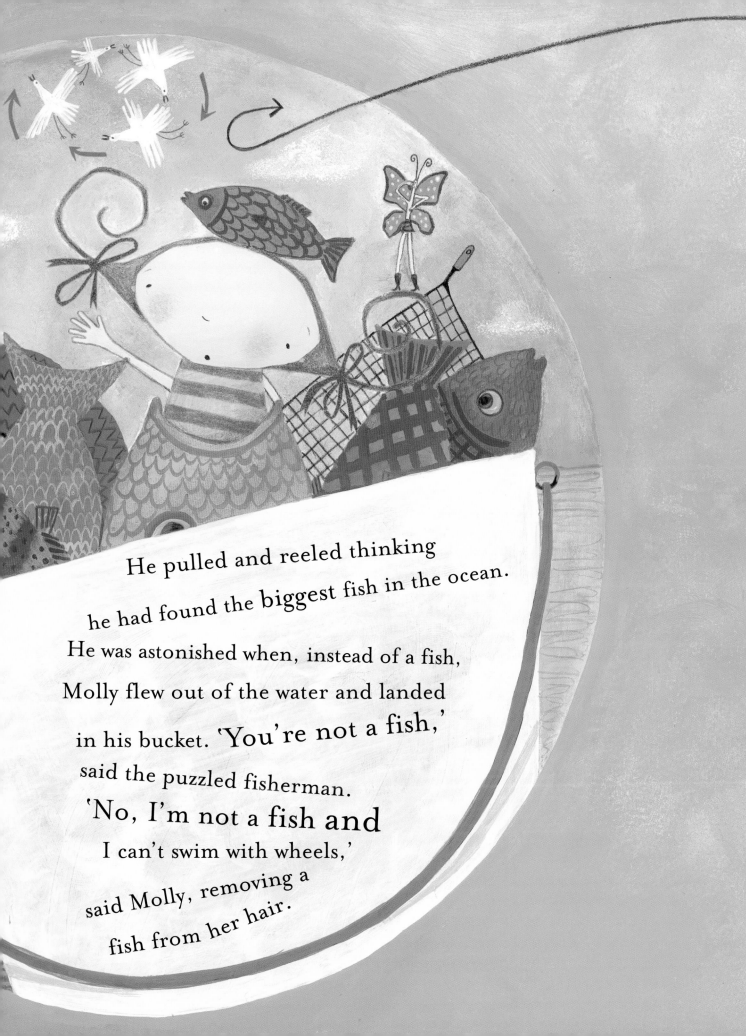

He pulled and reeled thinking

he had found the biggest fish in the ocean.

He was astonished when, instead of a fish,

Molly flew out of the water and landed

in his bucket. 'You're not a fish,'

said the puzzled fisherman.

'No, I'm not a fish and

I can't swim with wheels,'

said Molly, removing a

fish from her hair.

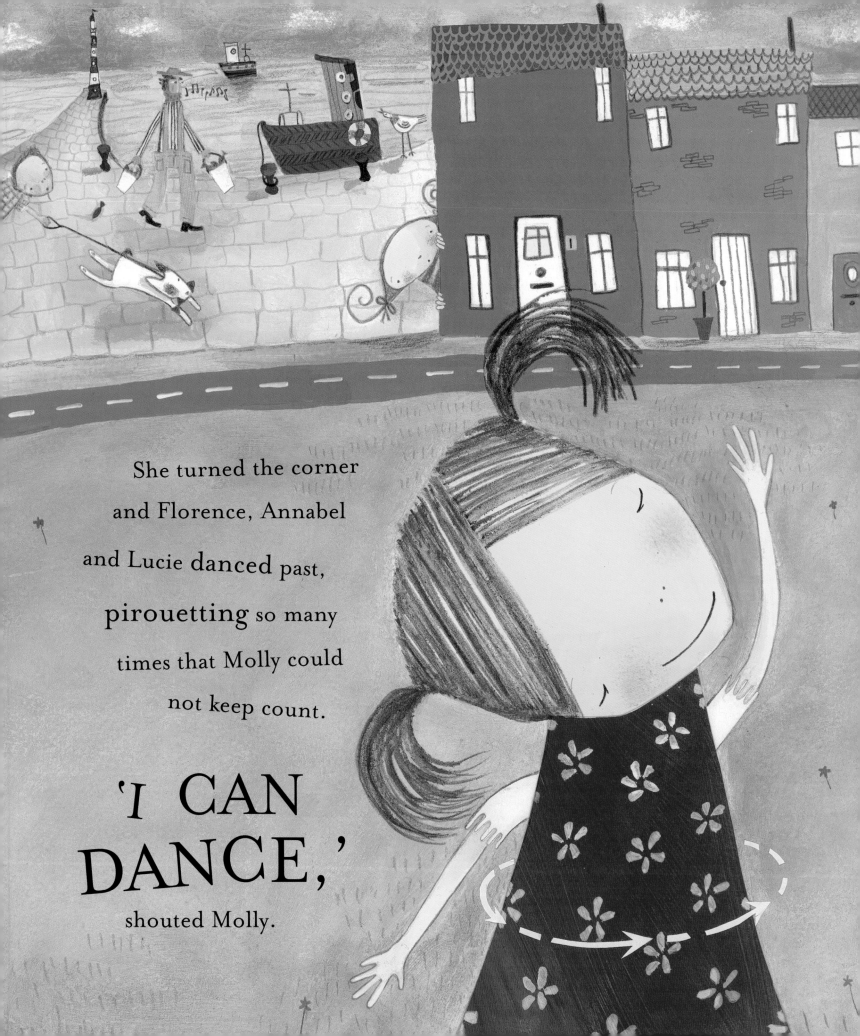

She turned the corner
and Florence, Annabel
and Lucie danced past,
pirouetting so many
times that Molly could
not keep count.

'I CAN
DANCE,'
shouted Molly.

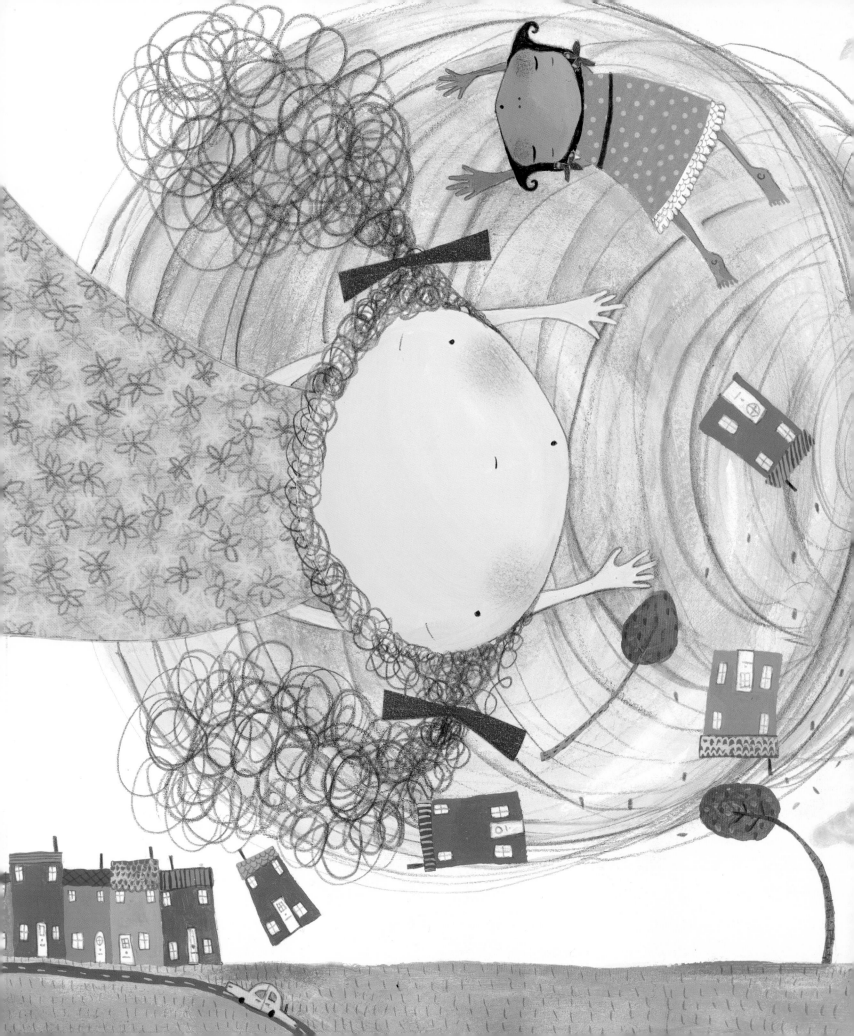

But her wheels spun so fast and so quick that soon she was completely out of control.

Eventually
she stopped spinning
and landed with a **thump**
in the middle of the park.

She began to get up,
when she heard a loud

'Hiyaaa'.

Billy was practising his karate kicks.

He could kick through the air
as swift as an arrow.

'I can do that,'
said Molly,
and she launched herself
into the air.

'MIND
OUT
FOR
THE—'

called Billy.

But

it was too late.

Molly kicked

a large beehive

and thirty angry bees came swarming straight towards her.

three times.

twice,

once,

They buzzed and chased her round the park:

Finally, Molly hid behind the large park notice board
and the bees went buzzing on ahead.

Drifting over from the other side of
the board came Archie's voice:

'Quick, quick,
catch him,'
he shouted.

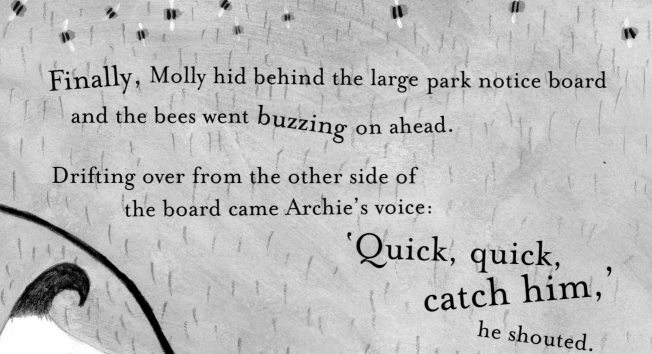

'I can't climb trees or swim, dance or
karate kick, and I certainly can't
catch Rufus,' Molly grumbled.

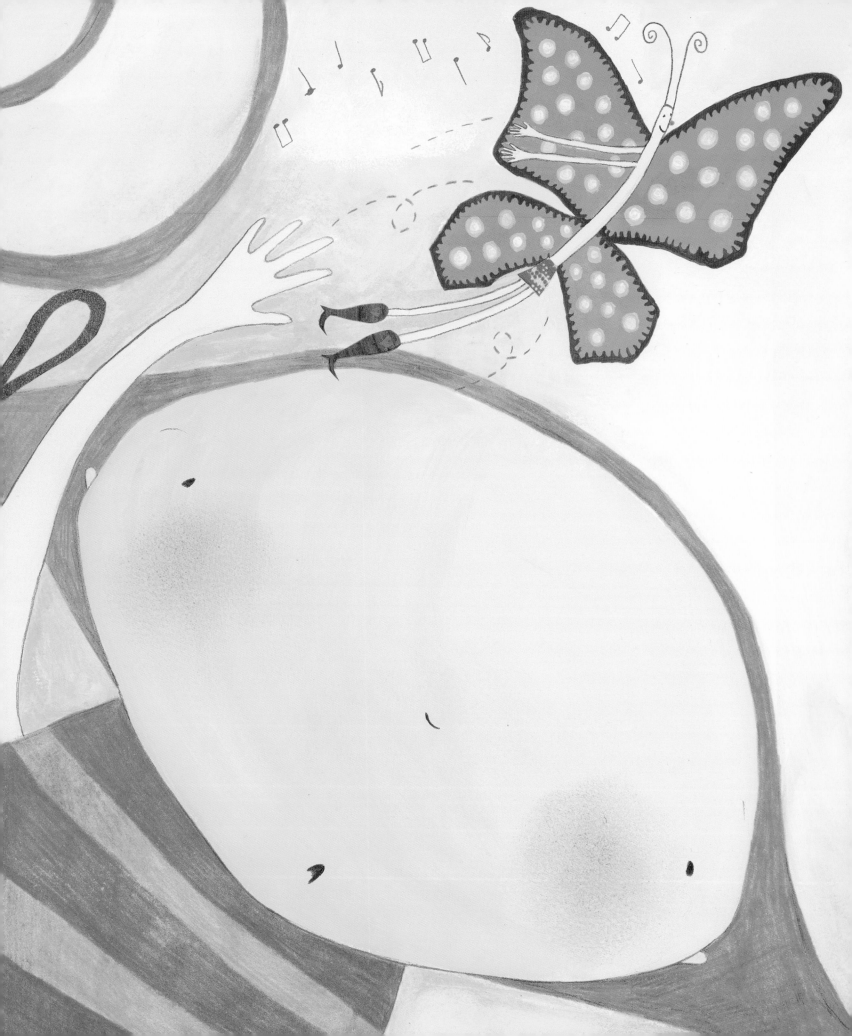

Just
then the butterfly
fluttered past Molly's nose.
'Butterfly, you were wrong,
I can't do anything,'
shouted Molly, running after
the butterfly.

She was concentrating so hard
on catching up with the butterfly
that she did not realise she had
overtaken the other children
one by one and within a few
seconds had caught up with Rufus.

Rufus' lead entangled itself in one of
Molly's wheels and they tumbled and
rolled down to the bottom of the hill.
The other children were running so fast
that they toppled head over heels joining
Molly and Rufus in one enormous heap.

'You've done it,
you've done it,' sang the
butterfly.
'You've caught Rufus.'

'Your wheels
are
wheely fast!'
cried the other children.

Molly grinned.
'So I am good at something,'
she said.
'I like my wheels
after all.'

Dedicated, with butterfly kisses, to my family and to my God, the prince of peace.

The right of Miriam Latimer to be identified as the author and illustrator of this Work has been asserted by her in accordance with the Copyright, Designs and Patents Act 1988.

Published by Hodder Children's Books, a division of Hodder Headline Limited, 338 Euston Road, London NW1 3BH. Printed in China. All rights reserved.

WHEELIE GIRL
by Miriam Latimer

British Library Cataloguing in Publication Data.

A catalogue record of this book is available from the British Library.

ISBN 0 340 88415 0 (HB). Copyright © Miriam Latimer 2006.

First published 2006. 10 9 8 7 6 5 4 3 2 1